# DR. WAYNE W. DYER

with Kristina Tracy

# Incredible You!

10 ways to let your GREATNESS shine through

HAY HOUSE, INC.
Carlsbad, California
New York City
London • Sydney
Johannesburg
Vancouver • Hong Kong
New Delhi

illustrated by
Melanie Siegel

*Published and distributed in the United States by:* Hay House, Inc.: www.hayhouse.com® • *Published and distributed in Australia by:* Hay House Australia Pty. Ltd.: www.hayhouse.com.au • *Published and distributed in the United Kingdom by:* Hay House UK, Ltd.: www.hayhouse.co.uk • *Published and distributed in the Republic of South Africa by:* Hay House SA (Pty), Ltd.: www.hayhouse.co.za • *Distributed in Canada by:* Raincoast: www.raincoast.com • *Published in India by:* Hay House Publishers India: www.hayhouse.co.in

Design: Jenny Richards • Illustrations: ©Melanie Siegel

Library of Congress Control Number: 2005925315

ISBN 13: 978-1-4019-0782-2
ISBN 10: 1-4019-0782-2

15  14  13  12      9  8  7  6

1st printing, October 2005
6th printing, June 2012

Printed in China

# Contents

# Introduction

I've been writing books designed to help people realize their own magnificence, while overcoming any and all self-imposed limitations, for the past 35 years. While these books have largely targeted adult populations, the essential message applies to all of us, from infancy on up.

A few years ago I wrote a book called *10 Secrets for Success and Inner Peace*. I created it so that my own teenage children would have a message in one place from their father that contained the ten most important ideas and practices they might choose to adopt for living a happy, fulfilled life.

In *this* book, I've taken those same ten ideas and framed them for the youngest of those among us. I believe that you cannot start early enough to teach the essential lessons for living a successful and peaceful life. In fact, I feel that reading these ideas and communicating them—even to your unborn child—makes perfect sense.

I've been reading children's books to young ones for as long as I can remember. My oldest daughter was born in 1967, and my youngest in 1989. I have a total of eight children and four grand-children, and reading to them at bedtime has been one of my all-time favorite blessings. It is my desire to have all of the children of the world grow up knowing within that they are indeed *incredible, divine beings.* This book was written and designed with this one idea in mind.

I've included several pages at the end of this book that contain questions and illustrations. When I read to my own small children, they loved it when we'd create our own story to match up with the drawings. Here, you can have your little angel answer the questions and participate in creating his or her own version of what to say in response to these colorful and imaginative drawings.

It is my desire to have these tiny, precious souls—so many of whom have brought so much joy into my life as they listened to my stories—close this book and feel so good about themselves that they feel in their hearts that nothing is impossible for them. It would be even more thrilling for me if this becomes the book they choose each night . . . so that a special person—like you—can read it to them over and over again.

I send you oceans of love.

— Wayne W. Dyer

There is good in you and in everyone.
Sharing this good with others is fun.
You have so many ideas inside your mind.
Set them free; you are one of a kind.

Dog Treats . . . . . 25¢
Water . . . . . 25¢
Balls . . . . . $1.00
All money goes to the County
★ Animal Shelter ★

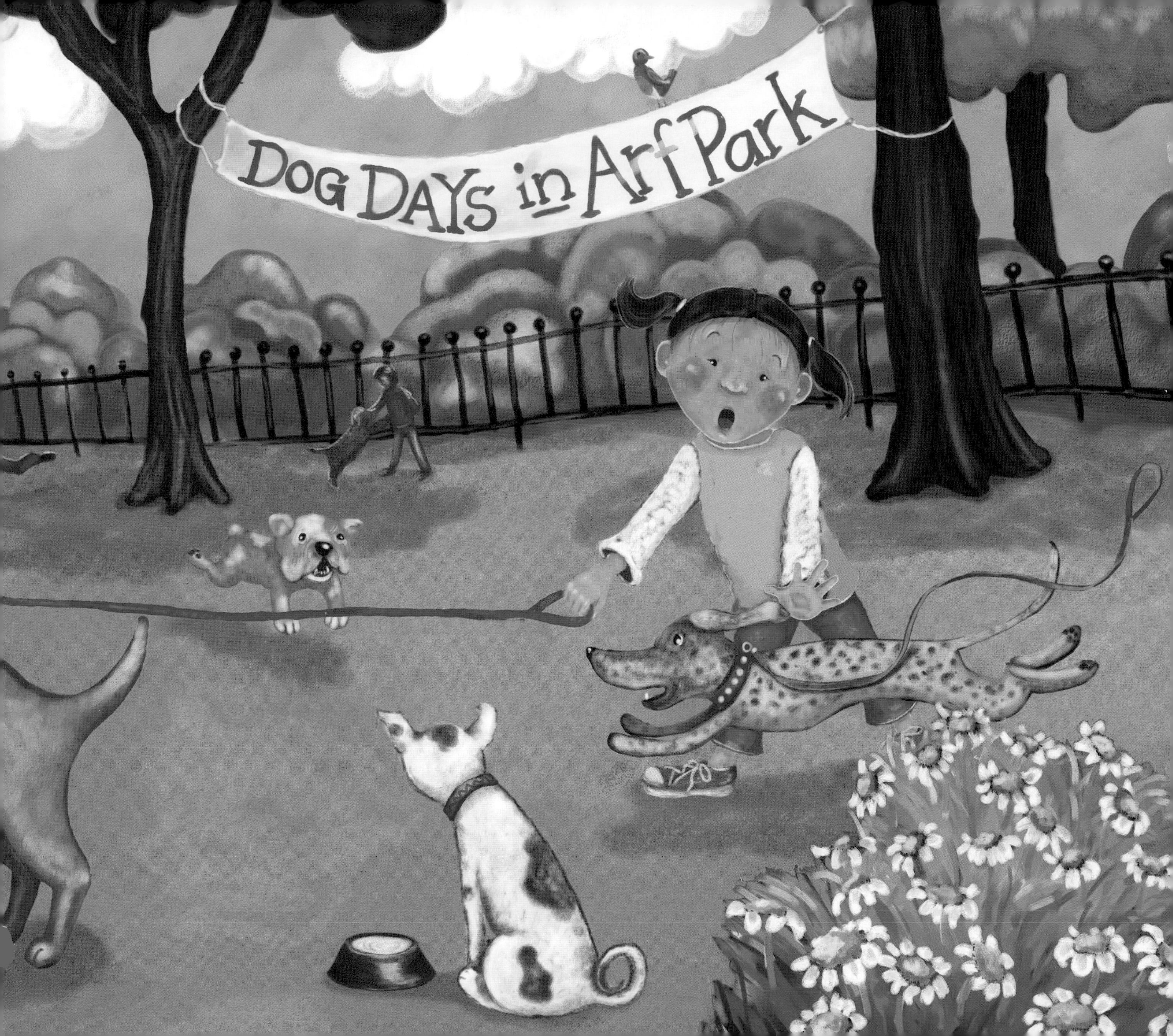
Dog Days in Arf Park

# #3 YOU ARE FILLED WITH LOVE

Your heart is like a magic cookie jar.
All the love you need is never far.

Think of something you love to do.
   That is your passion, so let it shine through.
Never let fear hold you back.
   Do what you love—you're on the right track.

So reach inside
and let that love out.
And it will come back to you
without a doubt.

Life can sometimes be so loud.
It's hard to listen with all those sounds!
Go to a quiet place inside.
There your mind
can wander
or just hide.

In your life, plenty has happened so far.
That's part of what makes you who you are.

But don't worry too much
about yesterday.
What matters is
what you do with today.

Some problems are big and some are small.
Thinking good thoughts can help you solve them all.

You can ask for help with what's bugging you. And never forget—
God is always there, too.

If something or someone makes you feel bad,
don't let it ruin your day by making you sad.
Let go of the hurt and take care of you.
You can't control what others say or do.

Pretend you are what you'd like to be.
Make a picture in your mind so you can see
that what you want can come true.
If you believe in your heart, it will come to you.

# #9 EVERYONE IS SPECIAL, ESPECIALLY YOU

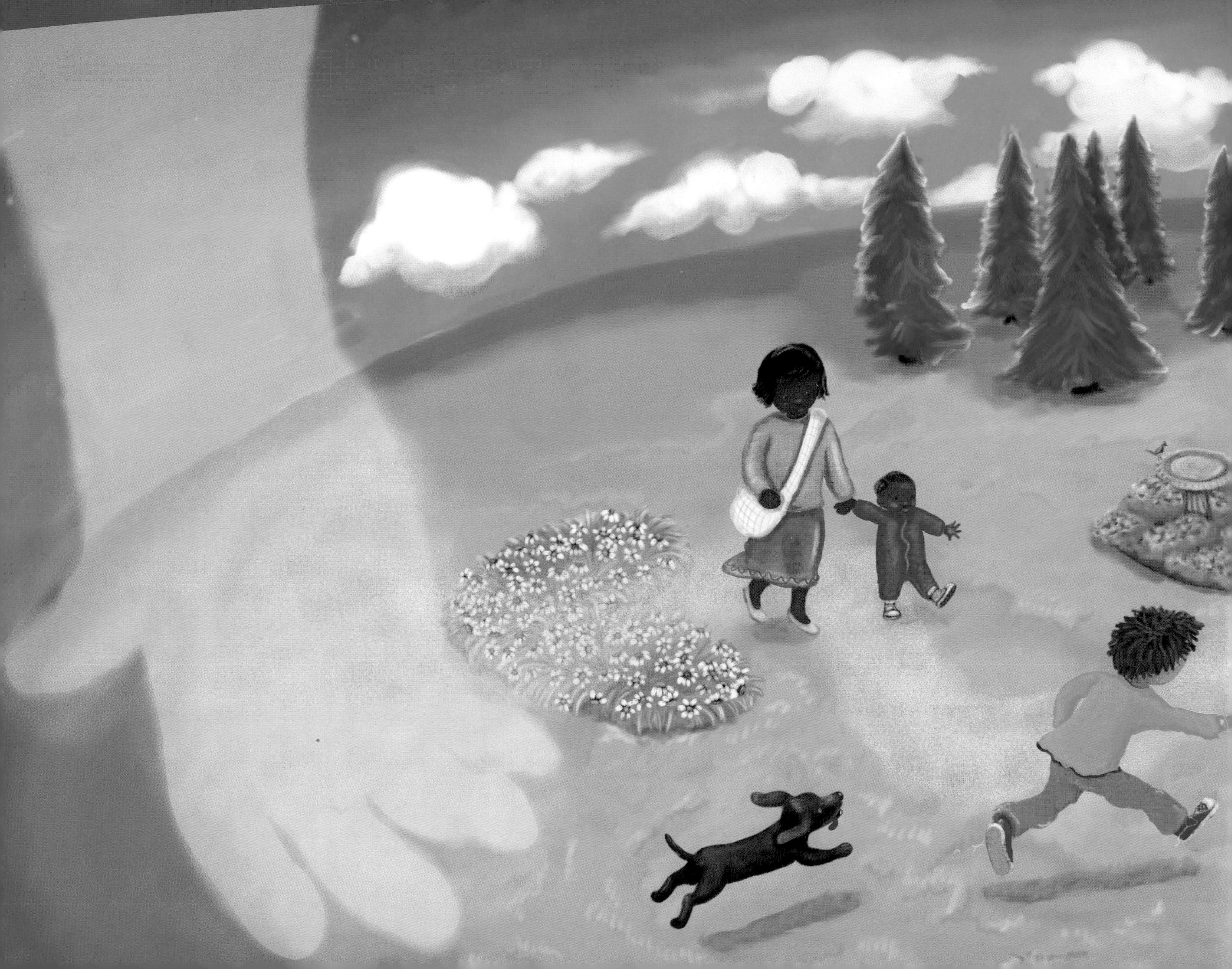

There's something on Earth that all people share.
It's the source of all good and love everywhere.
What is this great mystery, you may say?
It is God that connects us together this way!

Bad thoughts zap your energy.
Happy thoughts make you strong and free.
It's a choice you make each day,
so choose to be happy—that's the way!

I'M BRAVE!

I CAN! I'M SMART!

# What Do You Think?

Answer the questions on the following pages to learn how to use the ideas from this book in your own life. If you do, you will discover the most Incredible You!

**Q.** If someone or something makes you feel sad, embarassed, or angry, what do you do to make yourself feel better?

**Q.** Do you dream of doing something adventurous like taming lions? Or something that seems a little safer, like being a veterinarian? Close your eyes and imagine yourself doing it.

**Q.** What makes you feel scared or worried? What are some positive, strong words that you can say to yourself to overcome your fear?

**Q.** Everyone needs to be alone sometimes. Where do you go if you feel like being by yourself? To your room? Up in a tree? Or in a nice, comfy chair?

**Q.** If you have a problem or something is bothering you, who do you talk to? Your mom or dad? Your dog? Your teacher?

**Q.** It's important to make time for the things you love. Do you have a passion? Something you love to do more than anything else?

**Q.** What are some things you have done that make you great? Have you ever drawn an awesome picture that made you really proud? Have you ever won a medal or an award?

**Q.** Everyone is special and one-of-a-kind. What are some things you love about yourself, and how do you share that love with others? Do you bake cookies for your friends or pick flowers for your mom?

**Q.** These kids set up a stand to raise money for the animal shelter. What helpful ideas do you have inside your mind, and what can you do to share them with the world?

Dog Treats. . . . 25¢
Water. . . . . 25¢
Balls . . . . . $1.00
All money goes to the County
★ Animal Shelter ★

**Q.** Some people feel a loving Spirit around them. Some feel it in a church, a place of worship, or in nature. Do you feel this mysterious love that connects us all? Where?

We hope you enjoyed this Hay House book. If you'd like to receive our online catalog featuring additional information on Hay House books and products, or if you'd like to find out more about the Hay Foundation, please contact:

HAY
HOUSE

Hay House, Inc., P.O. Box 5100, Carlsbad, CA 92018-5100
(760) 431-7695 or (800) 654-5126
(760) 431-6948 (fax) or (800) 650-5115 (fax)
www.hayhouse.com® • www.hayfoundation.org

Published and distributed in Australia by: Hay House Australia Pty. Ltd., 18/36 Ralph St., Alexandria NSW 2015 • Phone: 612-9669-4299 • Fax: 612-9669-4144 • www.hayhouse.com.au

Published and distributed in the United Kingdom by: Hay House UK, Ltd., 292B Kensal Rd., London W10 5BE • Phone: 44-20-8962-1230 • Fax: 44-20-8962-1239 • www.hayhouse.co.uk

Published and distributed in the Republic of South Africa by: Hay House SA (Pty), Ltd., P.O. Box 990, Witkoppen 2068 • Phone/Fax: 27-11-467-8904 • www.hayhouse.co.za

Published in India by: Hay House Publishers India, Muskaan Complex, Plot No. 3, B-2, Vasant Kunj, New Delhi 110 070 • Phone: 91-11-4176-1620 • Fax: 91-11-4176-1630 • www.hayhouse.co.in

Distributed in Canada by: Raincoast, 9050 Shaughnessy St., Vancouver, B.C. V6P 6E5 • Phone: (604) 323-7100 • Fax: (604) 323-2600 • www.raincoast.com

**Take Your Soul on a Vacation**

Visit www.HealYourLife.com® to regroup, recharge, and reconnect with your own magnificence. Featuring blogs, mind-body-spirit news, and life-changing wisdom from Louise Hay and friends.

Visit www.HealYourLife.com today!